GLORIA HOUSTON

Littlejim's Gift
An Appalachian Christmas Story

illustrated by THOMAS B. ALLEN

Philomel Books ❖ New York

Library of Congress Cataloging-in-Publication Data
Houston, Gloria. Littlejim's gift/Gloria Houston; illustrated by Thomas B. Allen.
p.   cm.   Summary: While hoping to convince his stern father that he will soon be a man,
almost-eleven-year-old Littlejim uses his hard-earned savings for his sister's Christmas gift.
[1. Christmas—Fiction. 2. Family life—Fiction. 3. Fathers and sons—Fiction.]
I. Allen, Thomas B., ill. II. Title. III. Title: Littlejim's gift
PZ7.H8184Lk 1994 [Fic]—dc20 93-41736 CIP AC ISBN 0-399-22696-6

1   3   5   7   9   10   8   6   4   2
First Impression

To my wonderful nephew, Jordan Thompson Houston.—G.H.

In memory of my mother, Helen Frances Burt.—T.B.A.

Chinquapin winter had come to the Creek. The days shimmered in the glow of leaves painted by first frost, but lengthening shadows were cast by the twin peaks the Indians had long ago called the Spear Tops. The nights were cold, and the scent of winter was on the wind.

That's what Bigjim, his papa, told Littlejim as they banked the cabbage heads in soil at the edge of the garden during last twilight.

"Papa, will you let us go to the Christmas tree this year?" Littlejim asked as they spread the soil around the cabbage stalks.

"No time for funning and frolicking," the tall man answered through the mustache that framed his face almost covered by a slouch hat. "A full-growed man has no time for funning. You'll know that soon enough."

"Mama says Christmas feels so wonderful," said Littlejim. "Why don't we celebrate Christmas like other folks? Mama says her Fadde even let her family have a Christmas tree in their house in the old country!"

"No time for celebrating. Most of our boys from off the Creek here are across the water trying to whup the Kaiser. What with the war and all, Christmas is just another day. And that's that," said his father.

Bigjim's word was final. He was the best logger on the Creek, and everybody looked up to him. But Bigjim was hard on his only son.

"Seems I can't do anything to please him," Littlejim told Mama.

"Yah, your papa is a hard man," said Mama. "But he surely loves us all. He works so hard for us. But he forgets you are not yet a man."

Every night Littlejim snuggled under the pretty quilt Mama made for him and dreamed he would soon be man enough to please Papa.

In his dream he heard his papa say, "You're finally a full-growed man, my son. You are old enough to learn to use the tools." Then Bigjim would hand him the keys to the toolshed. But Littlejim knew that would never happen, although the boy wanted to learn to build things more than almost anything else. There was little time for his papa to teach him woodworking. Bigjim's logging often took him away from the farm on the Creek, and so there was no way Littlejim could prove himself to his papa.

Then one day he saw something in the window at Burleson's store that changed his dream: a set of tools fashioned to fit hands that were not yet a man's. The sight brought a smile to the boy's lips. Littlejim's heart beat at the thought of owning his own tools. If only he had his own hammer and saw, he could show Papa he was a man. From that day on Littlejim saved his every penny.

The weeks passed and one day later that fall, when the colors of the maple danced against the window in the upstairs sleeping room, Littlejim took the stone from its chink in the fireplace. Carefully he set it on the floor of the sleeping loft, and reached in to lift out the Half-and-Half tobacco can Uncle Bob had given him.

"Sixty. Seventy. Eighty. Almost enough," he whispered. "I have almost enough to buy them."

Just then Mama called up the stairs. "Jimmy. Jimmy, the eggs and butter are on the sled. Time to go to the store in Plumtree."

"Coming, Mama," said Littlejim. He hurried to replace the can in its hiding place.

Littlejim and his younger sister Nell trekked the three miles along the Creek Road toward the village of Plumtree, their mittened hands sharing the pulling rope by turns. At the forks, where Henson Creek Road met the River Road, Preacher Hall from the Missionary Baptist Church howdied them and gave them a ride in his new buggy. "I hear that the school's having a Bible verse competition. The winner will recite the winning verses for us at the Christmas tree. Are you going to enter, Littlejim?" the preacher asked.

"The winner *has* to go to the Christmas tree?" asked Littlejim.

"That's what I hear," said the preacher.

"Then, I'm entering the competition," said Littlejim.

Around the turn they could see Burleson's store, its white front like the frosting on one of Mama's cakes against the dark Blue Ridge Mountains.

Littlejim led his sister by the hand through the crowded storeyard and pushed the little sled under the hitching posts out of the way of the horses tied there. He gave Nell the basket of eggs. Then he lifted the pails of butter, one in each hand.

They trudged up the steps and across the wide front porch. Nell stopped with a catch of her breath.

"There it is," said Nell. "Do you see it, Littlejim?" Her eyes were shining. She stood on tiptoe.

Hanging on a wooden rack in the middle of the window was a beautiful doll. Its chalk-white face had two blue eyes, pink lips, and brown curls that looked like Nell's. Its long blue dress and fancy bonnet were trimmed with lace and tiny white ribbons. A tiny brown fur muff and tiny leather shoes made the doll look very rich. Next to the doll lay the metal box holding the woodworking tools Littlejim longed to have for his very own.

"That's a mighty fearful job, Littlejim," said Mr. Burleson. "I don't know as I would let a boy of mine do that. You be careful, son."

"I can handle it," said Littlejim. "I'll turn eleven next month. I'm almost a man." He looked out the window and into Nell's face. She was standing on the porch, gazing with longing at the doll.

"I guess Nell wants that doll something awful," he thought. "I guess she wants it as much as I want the tool set."

"Bigjim know what a fine boy he's got, son?" asked Mr. Burleson. "Fine boy working for his Uncle Bob at the sawmill ought to own that fine set of tools, don't you think?"

Littlejim stood as tall as he could. Mr. Burleson grinned and patted the boy on the shoulder. Mr. Burleson said, "Miss Gertrude's order is ready. You better start home. The old woman's picking her geese today. Already spitting snow. Be shoetop high by the time you young'uns make the Creek."

Mr. Burleson walked with Littlejim through the big front doors to meet Nell. At the hitching post, he helped the children pack the sugar, coffee, thread, and cocoa into the sled. Then Littlejim took Nell's mittened hand. Their shoes made half-moons on either side of the straight ribbons formed by the runners of the sled as they began their long trek back to the Henson Creek Road.

Every Saturday morning Littlejim hurried to the sawmill at sunup. His job as dust-doodler was to push the heavy wheelbarrow filled with sawdust and wood shavings out of the pit, with the big circle saw whining only inches above his head. And every Saturday evening, Uncle Bob gave him a shiny new dime to add to his stash.

But this Saturday was different. Bigjim wakened his son before the sun was up.

"Fayette's down his back," Bigjim said. "You ain't much of a man, but I need you to help me in the woods."

"A chance to prove I am a man," said Littlejim to the mirror over the washbasin on the back porch. "I'll work so hard he won't have any doubt."

All day the wind screamed down the northy holler. Scott and Swain, Bigjim's matched Percherons, stamped their huge hooves on the snow and snorted, their breath making smoke in the wind.

Bigjim chopped off the lower limbs of a tall spruce tree.

The man handed his son one end of the crosscut saw. They placed it inside the cut the ax had made. Back and forth. Back and forth. The saw pulled at the muscles in Littlejim's arms. It was hard work, but Littlejim wanted Papa to see how strong he was. So he pulled harder.

The smell of pine resin made his nose tickle as Littlejim stood back from the trunk to watch the tree fall.

Slowly, like a lurching giant trying hard to stay on his feet, the heavy green branches swayed. They filled the woods with a swishing sound. Finally a crack like a rifle shot echoed from one holler to another and back. The huge log thudded to the ground, bounced, and lay still.

When dinnertime came at midday, the lard buckets that held Mama's ham biscuits and fried apple pies were frozen solid.

"We'll eat back at the house tonight," said Bigjim. "No dinner this noon."

The two worked on through the afternoon. Littlejim's stomach was so empty it began to gnaw at his backbone. Sweat dripped down his back under his wool underwear, but his feet were numb from the cold. His hands were shaking.

He took off his mittens and blew on his hands to warm them.

"Jimmy!" shouted Bigjim. "Get that header-grab!"

Littlejim leaped forward to catch the iron tool with both hands. His mittens fell through the branches. As his numb hands touched the cold metal, they burned, just like touching Mama's black cookstove when it was hot.

Pain seared his arms to his shoulders. Littlejim fell into a bed of pine branches. He smelled the fragrance of the needles as he fainted.

When he awoke his face was resting against the scratchy wool of Papa's coat. He could hear the clip-clop of Swain's hooves jostling as they rode to Doctor Sloop's office. He could barely see the sign DR. MARY SLOOP over the door. The next thing he knew he could see himself reflected in the lady's glasses as she and a girl Littlejim's age soothed cool ointment on his hands.

"You're in my class," he said to the girl. "Your name is Emma."

"Sh-h-h-h," Dr. Mary whispered. "Sleep, Jimmy."

Mama met them at the door and tucked Littlejim into the trundle bed in the front bedroom where Mama and Bigjim slept. His hands were bandaged so he looked like the drawings of the prizefighters in Papa's *Kansas City Star*.

At first his hands hurt so much he wanted to cry. Even Mama's rich potato soup was not as good as usual. But each day, he grew stronger and his hands hurt less and less.

Finally he was able to read the books Mr. Osk sent him from school. Every day he studied his verses for the competition at the school, and every day after school Nell brought Littlejim a surprise. One day she brought the sadiron and a hammer to crack his favorite hickory nuts, which she fed him carefully one by one. Another day she found an empty hornet's nest and put it on the table beside the bed. Sometimes she struggled to read aloud to him. Every day she sat at his feet and listened as he recited his verses.

"You know so many, Littlejim!" she told her older brother adoringly. "I know you're going to win the recitation contest."

"I hope so," he said.

"And then Papa will have to let us go to the Christmas tree. Do you think we'll get a present, Littlejim? I pray every night for a china-head doll," said Nell.

"I don't know, but don't worry, Nell," said Littlejim. He tried to pat his little sister's hand, but he only hit her with his bandage.

As he lay in the big bed he sometimes thought about the little tool set in the window at Burleson's store. He only needed two more dimes to buy it. But every time he thought about the tools, he could see Nell's face filled with longing as she looked at the doll. And he remembered all the nice things she had done for him while his hands healed. Finally he told Mama about his plan.

"Mama, will you keep a secret for me?" he asked.

"Yah, of course. What is the secret?"

He told her about his stash of dimes in the tobacco can in the hidey-hole behind the chink in the chimney. Mama brought the can of dimes and poured them on the quilted comforter on Littlejim's knees.

"What a sum of money you have saved, my little Jimmy," Mama said. "But let's keep the dimes. When you are well you can buy something you really want," said Mama. But all Littlejim could see in his mind was his sister's face as it looked through the store window at the doll.

"Mama," said Littlejim, "every day Nell has helped me learn the verses. As soon as my hands are well, I want to buy the beautiful doll in Burleson's store window for her. Will you take me to the store one day before we go to the Christmas tree at the church?"

"That is very generous of you, Jimmy," said Mama. "It is the true spirit of Christmas." Mama leaned down to kiss her son's hair and added, "And we *will* go to the Christmas tree at the church this year. No matter what James allows." Mama reminded Littlejim of one of her Dominiquer hens with its feathers ruffled when she got mad at her tall husband.

The day of the recitations, Littlejim was the last to walk to the platform. He had learned his verses so well that everyone who heard him said they could see the Baby and the shepherds and the wise men in the village of Bethlehem.

When all the recitations at the school were finished, Mr. Osk, the teacher, took off his glasses and wiped his eyes with his big handkerchief. Then he announced, "For a moment there we were all transported back to Bethlehem, I believe. Littlejim, you will give the recitation at the Christmas tree this year at the Missionary Baptist Church."

"Now we will go to the Christmas tree," Littlejim told his mama that night.

"Yah, we will go to the Christmas tree this year," said Mama.

On the morning of Christmas Eve, Mama hitched Scott and Swain to the wagon, and drove her son to Burleson's store. There he spent all of his dimes for the beautiful doll with the china head. Then Mama drove the wagon to Mr. Osk's house so Littlejim could ask his teacher to take the doll to the church. Nell would be very surprised when the doll was on the Christmas tree.

At supper Mama announced in an important-sounding voice, "James, our son is the winner of the competition at the school. He will recite his verses at the Christmas tree tonight. Osk has asked us to join him. Will you go?"

Bigjim glowered across the supper table, but he said nothing to his tiny wife.

"Then *we* will go," she said. "We will go with you, or without you."

Littlejim, Nell, and Baby May sat very still until Bigjim got up, took his hat off the peg by the door and went outside.

"Time to go to the Christmas tree," said Mama, with a bright smile. "With Papa or without him."

Mama, Littlejim, Nell, and Baby May rode to the church with Mr. Osk in his buggy.

Littlejim looked around the church. An enormous mountain laurel, the kind the outlanders called rhododendron, filled the front corner of the little church. Its broad green leaves were lighted with hundreds of tiny red candles. Strings of popcorn and cranberries wove their way among the branches.

Tied to the lower branches were presents wrapped in colored paper and tied with colored string. Members of the families who lived on the Creek would exchange gifts after the program. Presents had been carefully made or purchased for the person whose name was on the tiny strip of paper each member of the congregation had pulled from the preacher's black hat at last Sunday's service.

Mama, Littlejim, Nell, and Baby May sat on the women and children's side of the aisle. Mr. Osk went to sit with the church leaders in the Amen corner.

If only Papa could see how beautiful it all was, his son was sure that he would decide that celebrating Christmas was a good thing to do.

"Is this how Christmas feels, Mama?" said Littlejim.

"This is how Christmas feels, Jimmy."

"I'm sorry Papa isn't feeling it too," Littlejim added.

"Maybe someday he will," Mama replied.

When it was time for Littlejim to recite, he began, "For unto us a child is born, unto us a son is given; and the government shall be upon his shoulder; and his name shall be called Wonderful, Counsellor, the mighty God, the everlasting Father, the Prince of Peace...."

Littlejim looked to the corner of the room where Mama and Nell were sitting.

He continued, "And when they had opened their treasures, they presented unto him gifts; gold, and frankincense, and myrrh...."

After he had finished, Littlejim went to sit with Mama and Nell. Soon it would be time for the most exciting part of the Christmas tree at the church—the time when the presents would be given out.

The double doors opened. Several of the older boys stood with big lard buckets filled with small brown paper sacks. Every person attending the Christmas tree program would receive one.

Preacher Hall stood up. "St. Nicholas will need some helpers to pass out the pokes of candy. Any volunteers?" Every hand on the children's side of the aisle shot up.

Then the doors opened again. A short round man wearing a long red cape, peaked hat, and a white beard came through the doors.

"St. Nicholas looks mighty like Mr. Burleson," Littlejim whispered to Mama.

Nell stared at the figure with her eyes wide and her mouth open.

The caped figure handed out several switches from his bag to the older boys on the children's side of the aisle. Then he went to the deacons in the Amen corner, a place of honor where the important church leaders usually sat solemnly nodding until one of them felt moved by the preacher's words to shout "A-a-a-men!" St. Nicholas handed each of the deacons a lump of coal or a willow switch. The adults laughed because lumps of coal were given only to those who had misbehaved during the year, and everyone knew the deacons were much too important to misbehave.

Then St. Nicholas helped the volunteers hand out the Christmas treat pokes to the older men and women seated around the stove. Each of the children received a small brown bag, too. At last, the adults received their treats.

Finally it was time to hand out the gifts tied on the tree, the gifts from families and friends. St. Nicholas asked the children to sit down. Then Mr. Osk, Littlejim's teacher, and Cousin Tarp helped St. Nicholas hand out the gifts.

St. Nicholas untied each gift from the tree and read the names in loud tones. One of the two men delivered the gift to the person whose name was called. "Nell. Nell Houston," called St. Nicholas.

He walked over to the pew where she sat. St. Nicholas handed Nell the doll. Her face glowed as she smoothed the lace on the doll's dress.

Littlejim looked into his treat poke so Mama wouldn't see the tears of happiness in his eyes. He took out a red-and-white-striped stick of peppermint candy, then pulled out an orange, and two pieces of taffy wrapped in colored paper. He tasted the peppermint stick, and looked at the fat Christmas laurel with its twinkling candles. "Christmas feels so very good, Mama. I'm glad I used my dimes to buy the doll for Nell," he whispered.

"I'm glad also," said Mama, hugging her son to her side.

"Jimmy. Littlejim Houston," St. Nicholas was saying. "Present here for Littlejim Houston. Anybody here by that name?"

Startled, Littlejim looked at St. Nicholas. The bearded man handed him a long flat parcel wrapped in white paper and tied with red string. He looked at the package in his hands. Littlejim knew what was wrapped inside. He had seen it in Burleson's store window.

"Your butter and egg money...." whispered Littlejim. "That's what you did with it, isn't it? But how did you know?"

"Mr. Burleson told me of your wish," said Mama. "The spirit of love should be rewarded. Merry Christmas, Jimmy."

"Move over, son," said a deep bass voice above Littlejim's head.

Bigjim was standing there wearing his Sunday-go-to-meeting shirt and necktie.

"Our son is quite a man, don't you agree, James?" said Mama.

"Almost a man," grunted Bigjim, as he placed his arm around Littlejim's shoulder.

The choirmaster doh-sol-me-dohed to tune up the choir, and the congregation began to sing.

"When the roll is called up yonder," sang Bigjim.

Littlejim could feel his voice deepen as he joined his papa.

"When the roll is called up yonder, I'll be there," sang Littlejim, his voice blending with his papa's.

"Papa," he whispered. "Doesn't Christmas feel good?"

"Hur-umph," grunted Bigjim when the song ended. "Just another day." But his hand squeezed Littlejim's shoulder, and his bass voice was filled with joy and pride.

Nell peeked around Mama's arm and smiled at her brother, hugging her beautiful doll.

Littlejim was snuggled in between his mama and his papa. The smell of pine and candles, the warm feel of his papa's arm on his shoulder, the cool metal of the little toolbox in his hand joined the happiness Littlejim felt inside.

His heart was filled. His happiness was bigger than the Christmas laurel. It filled the little church house, maybe it even filled the whole world.